Sandy Lane
Stables
and the
surrounding area

SANDY
BAY

BUCKNELL
WOODS

ASH HILL

To
COLCOTT

PIG
FARM

Sandy Lane Stables

Sandy Lane Stables

A Star at the Stables

Michelle Bates

Adapted by: Megan Cullis

Reading consultant: Alison Kelly

Series editor: Lesley Sims

Designed by: Brenda Cole

Cover and inside illustrations: Barbara Bongini and Ian McNee

Map illustrations: John Woodcock

First published in 2017 by Usborne Publishing Ltd.,
Usborne House, 83-85 Saffron Hill, London EC1N 8RT, England.
www.usborne.com

Contents

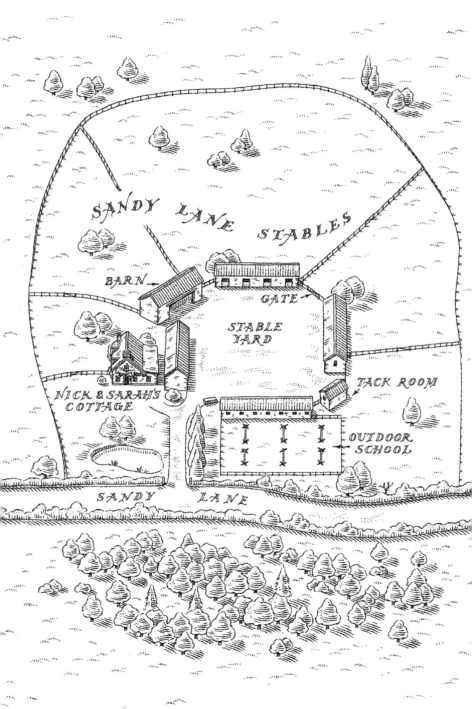

Chapter 1

The Arrival

"Not bad, Jess," Tom Buchanan called from the middle of the outdoor school. "But you rushed the parallel bars a bit. Try to take a little more time in the approach – give Skylark a chance to see what she's jumping."

"Rushed the parallel bars a bit?" Jess Adams whispered to her best friend, Rosie Edwards. "Who does Tom think he is?"

The midday jumping practice at Sandy Lane Stables was well underway and, as the summer sun beat down on the horses and their riders, Jess cantered her pony around the outdoor school one more time, before trotting over to join her friends.

"Oh, come on, Jess," Rosie said, catching Jess making a face at Tom. "Tom's only trying to help. He's under a lot of pressure at the moment, what with his instructor's exams coming up."

"I guess," Jess replied, leaning down to pat Skylark's dappled grey neck.

With Tom's exams a few weeks away, it was hardly surprising that he was taking the practices so seriously. If he passed them he'd become a qualified riding instructor.

Jess sighed. She had to admit that she was probably more cross with herself than Tom. The Colcott Horse Show was in just two weeks, and she knew how much work she still had to put in with Skylark. Tom reminding her of that fact only made it worse. He was right. She had rushed her pony at the parallel bars.

It was Rosie's turn next. Jess watched as she turned Midnight to the course. Neatly, they cantered towards the brush hurdle, popping over the first jump with ease. Then Rosie turned the black thoroughbred for the gate, her long, blonde hair flying out behind her. Jess held her breath as Rosie leaned forward in the approach. Midnight rose carefully for the jump, soared through the air and touched down again. Jess let out a low whistle. Rosie was such a relaxed rider... Jess wished she could be so together herself.

Now, Rosie was collecting Midnight in-hand for the staircase. Flying through the air, they cleared the jump with feet to spare, before turning for the double. *One... two...* Jess counted the strides in her head. Then they were over that and on to the shark's teeth. Rosie cleared the final fence and drew Midnight to a halt.

"Not bad, Rosie." Tom smiled. "Now, as we've all ridden the course, we'll take these horses back to the yard and get everything tidied up before our guests arrive."

Jess looked across at Rosie and grinned. News

had spread fast that a film was being shot on location at a big country estate just down the road from Sandy Lane. Jess and Rosie had already cycled down to have a sneaky look at the set. They'd even spotted some actors wandering about in Victorian costumes.

And, as if that wasn't exciting enough, Nick and Sarah Brooks, the owners of Sandy Lane, had announced that Sarah was going to be teaching the American teen actor, Bella Ford, to ride side-saddle. What was more, they had agreed to loan some of the Sandy Lane horses to the film set.

Nobody had been able to stop talking about it ever since. The film's producer – an old friend of Sarah's from when she'd lived in America – had already been to the stables to choose the mounts. That afternoon, Bella Ford herself was going to be visiting Sandy Lane to choose her pony and discuss a training programme with Sarah.

"So, what do you think she'll be like?" Rosie asked Jess, as the two girls turned their ponies through the gate and rode back up the driveway.

"Who?" Jess replied, nudging Skylark on.

"Bella Ford, silly," Rosie said.

"Oh her!" Jess grinned. "She'll probably walk right in here, want to be my best friend, then I won't want to know you any more."

Rosie rolled her eyes and laughed. "Jess Adams, I don't know why I put up with you."

As the two girls rode back into the yard, Nick walked out of the tack room with a saddle under his arm, whistling a tune.

"Nick's in a good mood today," Jess mused.

Rosie nodded. "He's been like that all week."

It was hardly surprising. The film company was going to be paying Sandy Lane well and it couldn't have come at a better time. Nick and Sarah had been putting off doing any renovations to their cottage for ages, and then last winter the roof of the tack room had collapsed and everything had flooded, eating up their few savings. Extra money would certainly come in handy.

Jess jumped down from Skylark and led her to the

side of the yard, where she tied the pony's reins to a ring on the wall. She stood back to admire the little Arab, whose pebble-grey coat gleamed in the midday sun. She'd won Skylark in a competition – two years ago now – and in Jess's eyes there wasn't a pony in the world like her.

"All right, you." Jess grinned as Skylark nudged at her pockets. "I know you want to go out into the fields, but I have to clean you up first."

After dropping Skylark's saddle off in the tack room, she grabbed the hosepipe to fill up her bucket, and set about sponging her pony down.

Jess looked across at Rosie, who was already locked in concentration sponging Midnight's coat. Rosie was taking her grooming duties particularly seriously. Midnight's owner, Izzy Paterson, was away over the summer and Rosie had promised to look after him for her.

Smiling mischievously, Jess aimed the hosepipe at Rosie. "You look like you need a clean too, Rosie!"

Rosie shrieked as she got a face full of water. "I'll

get you for that!" Laughing, she threw her sponge at Jess and covered her in soapy suds. Soon, there were puddles of water everywhere, and the two friends fell about in hysterics.

"Enough, enough," Jess yelled, finally catching her breath.

It was into this scene of chaos that a sleek, black Mercedes rolled into the yard. For a second, Jess and Rosie just stood there. Then, dropping the hosepipe to the ground, Jess raced over to turn the water off.

The Mercedes purred to a stop, and a tall, thin woman climbed out of the front seat of the car. "We're here, darling," she said, peering across the yard through a pair of large sunglasses.

"OK Mother," came a voice from the car.

Jess looked at Rosie in panic, her face still dripping wet. "It's Bella Ford and her entourage," she whispered. "They're early!"

Chapter 2

Bella Ford

"I'll get Nick and Sarah," Rosie said, sprinting off across the yard in the direction of the cottage. Jess wiped her wet face with her sleeve, before hurrying over to welcome the new arrivals. There were three of them – the tall woman in sunglasses, a short, stocky man, and a pretty, dark-haired girl.

"Hello." Jess smiled, feeling surprisingly nervous. "I'm Jess, I ride here... well, ride and work... it's not really like working though," she gabbled. "My friend's just gone to get the owners."

"Nice to meet you, Jess," the man said kindly. "My

name's Rob Fraser. I'm a film producer. This is Bella Ford. No doubt you know who she is already." He winked, gesturing at the girl.

Bella gave Jess a bored look. "So this is Sandy Lane Stables?" she sniffed, looking around.

Jess watched Bella with curiosity. Was it just her, or did she sound a little... disdainful? A twinge of annoyance ran through her, but she tried hard to ignore it.

"Welcome to Sandy Lane!" Jess replied with as much enthusiasm as she could muster. "It doesn't look like much from the outside, but I promise you, you'll love it here!"

Bella pursed her lips and looked away.

Just then, Sarah crossed the yard carrying her two-year-old daughter, Zoe, on her hip.

"Hi there Rob." Sarah smiled. "Welcome back. Nick's just getting the horses ready for you."

"That's great." Rob gave a big grin. "Sarah – I'd like to introduce you to Bella Ford. And this is her mother, Miranda."

"Hello Miranda. Hi Bella." Sarah smiled warmly as she shook their hands. "Welcome to Sandy Lane Stables. I see you've already met Jess – she's one of our regulars!"

As Rob began to talk, Jess took a look at Bella. She looked about the same age and height as Jess, but that was where the similarities stopped. Dressed in a striped sailing top, a pair of white jeans and little navy pumps, Bella's style looked effortless. And, with her long, glossy brown hair and big green eyes, Jess could see in a second what made her a film star.

"We're all staying in a hotel in Ash Hill," Rob said, "and of course Bella has a trailer on site for her dressing room."

Jess nodded absent-mindedly as the conversation went on around her. But her eyes were focused on Bella, who had wandered across the yard towards Storm Cloud. Jess took a sharp breath – Bella was getting dangerously close to the pony's hindquarters, and she had a habit of lashing out.

"I wouldn't get too close," Jess said, dashing across

the yard towards Bella. She waited for Bella to turn around, but she ignored her.

"Look, I don't mean to be bossy," Jess started again. "It's just... Storm Cloud doesn't like anyone standing behind her."

Still Bella didn't move, and now the restless pony's tail was twitching back and forth. If Bella didn't get out of the way soon, Jess knew that she'd take an almighty kick.

Suddenly, Storm Cloud pawed at the ground and snorted. Without thinking, Jess flung herself at Bella, knocking her down.

"What on earth?" Sarah said, going over to the girls who lay tangled in a pool of muddy water.

"I-I'm sorry, Bella," Jess said, scrambling to her feet. She glanced at Sarah sheepishly. "I just... I thought... She was getting very close to Storm Cloud's back and you know how she can lash out..."

"You ridiculous girl," Bella cried, clambering up out of the puddle. "Look at the state of me!"

"Your gorgeous white jeans, darling!" Miranda

shrieked, clipping across the yard in her kitten heels.

"I'm really sorry... I– I–" Jess stuttered, noticing that Bella's crisp white jeans had turned a muddy shade of brown.

"Are you OK, Bella?" Sarah looked concerned.

"I would have been if it wasn't for *her*," Bella replied, scowling at Jess.

"Jess was only trying to help," Sarah explained. "Storm Cloud doesn't like it when people get too close to her hindquarters. She was badly treated by her previous owners and can be a bit sensitive." Jess shot Sarah a grateful look. "I'm sure it'll come out in the wash," Sarah went on. "It's only a bit of mud."

Just then, Nick's voice boomed out across the yard. Jess sighed with relief.

"Hello everyone!" he called, striding towards them all.

"Hi Nick." Rob smiled. "Good to see you again. This is Bella Ford and her mother, Miranda." Rob gestured at Miranda, who was too busy flicking bits of straw off Bella's arm to look up.

"Hey, are you OK? What happened to you?" Nick glanced at Bella's muddy jeans in surprise.

Bella scowled and ignored Nick's question.

There was an awkward pause before Nick spoke again. "Maybe it's time to take a look at the ponies?" he said, cheerily.

"Good idea," Rob replied. "Then we can talk about a training programme with Sarah. Bella is a good rider – that's why she does her own riding stunts – but she's never ridden side-saddle before."

"Well that shouldn't be a problem," Sarah said. "She should get the hang of it in no time."

Jess, who had been keeping quiet since her muddy encounter with Bella, looked at Sarah in admiration. Not only was Sarah a brilliant riding instructor, she'd also done some stunt work in America before she met Nick. Jess always loved hearing about her time working in film, and had even started to wonder if she could be a stunt rider one day herself.

"We've hired *Champion & Wilton* side-saddles," Rob went on. "Apparently they're the most authentic saddles for the period. Does that sound OK?"

"Weren't they produced seventy-odd years ago?" Sarah asked. "We'd have to be sure that they fitted the ponies, so they don't get saddle-sore."

"Sure," Rob said. "No problem. Anything that doesn't fit can be sent back."

"Can we just get on and choose my pony?" Bella whined. "I want to get this over with so I can get out of these horrible clothes."

"Yes, of course we can, Bella," said Rob. Jess thought she noticed a slight strain in his voice. "Is that OK with you, Nick?"

"Sure thing," Nick replied. "Come this way, folks." He led the group across the yard towards the stables. "You remember Hector, don't you Rob?" Nick said, as the sturdy bay gelding poked his head over the stable door. "He's one of the three mounts you've already chosen."

"Of course." Rob nodded approvingly.

"And Napoleon and Minstrel too," Nick said, pointing at the bay and the skewbald in the stables to his left. "And this is Pepper." Nick walked over to Pepper's stable, and fumbled around in his pocket for a sugar lump. Almost immediately, Pepper's nose appeared over the door. "He's very gentle so would probably be easy to train side-saddle."

"Eurgh, I don't want a piebald." Bella wrinkled up her nose.

"Well, what sort of pony do you want, Bella?" Nick said patiently.

"A grey," she said firmly. "I want to ride a grey."

"Then how about Feather?" Nick led them over to Feather's stable on the other side of the yard.

"She seems nice," Rob said, smiling earnestly.

"Oh no, I don't think so. Not pretty enough for my Bella," Miranda interrupted.

"Mother's right," Bella agreed. "I want something more... hmm... showy."

Jess caught Nick's eye and he raised an eyebrow.

"Well, what about Storm Cloud? She's a beauty!" he said, leading them across to the dappled grey pony tied up in the shade.

"Oh no." Bella grimaced. "I can't have a horse that kicks. What about that one over there?"

Jess turned around to see where Bella was pointing and her heart lurched. It was Skylark.

"I'm afraid Skylark's not available," Nick said quickly. "She's Jess's pony."

"Jess? Jess who?" Bella frowned.

"I'm Jess." Jess coughed nervously.

"I want that pony," Bella insisted, looking up at her mother. "Mother, take care of it for me."

"Of course, dear," Miranda cooed.

Rob looked at Nick awkwardly, then turned to Jess. "Do you think you would let us borrow her, Jess? She'd be perfect for the movie. We'd pay for her, of course."

Jess looked at Skylark and saw what Rob was seeing. With her delicately dished face, her perfect, long eyelashes and her fine black-rimmed eyes, Skylark was a film star pony in the making.

"You can have the use of any of the other ponies, just not this one," Nick insisted.

Jess noticed a slight look of panic in Nick's face. She knew what this film meant to Nick and Sarah – it would be a great thing for Sandy Lane. Plus, they had been so good to her over the years; they were like family. Jess took a deep breath.

"It's OK Bella, you can ride Skylark if you like," she said, quietly.

Nick looked completely taken aback. "Are you sure, Jess?"

Jess nodded.

"I think you should sleep on this." Sarah stepped in. "Letting someone else ride your pony is a huge decision for any owner to make. Besides, you've got the Colcott Show coming up." Sarah turned to Rob. "Our riders work hard all year round to take part in the circuit. If Jess lent her pony to Bella, she wouldn't be able to compete."

"It's all right," Jess said firmly. "This is more important than Colcott. Bella can ride her."

"Fantastic!" Rob beamed at Jess. "We really appreciate this, Jess. Don't we, Bella?"

Bella shrugged. "I guess so."

Sarah still looked uneasy. "Nick and I are really grateful, Jess. This is a big sacrifice to make."

Jess fought back the tears that were welling up in her eyes. *It's going to be a long summer ahead,* she thought. She knew it was the right thing to do, but the thought of giving Skylark to Bella for the whole summer was heartbreaking.

There was another awkward pause. Then Sarah spoke. "I suppose there is something we could do…" she said. "Jess, how would you feel about joining in with Bella's side-saddle training?"

Jess blinked, unsure she'd heard her correctly. *Side-saddle? With Sarah?* "Really?" she said.

Sarah nodded. "It would be a good discipline for you to learn. You know, learning to ride side-saddle was how I got into working in film." Sarah turned to Rob. "What do you think, Rob? Jess could train alongside Bella on another pony. To be honest, it would be easier for me to train two riders together."

"I don't see why not," Rob replied.

"Great." Sarah smiled. "So that's agreed. Jess, you can ride Storm Cloud for side-saddle training, while Bella is on Skylark."

Jess nodded. It meant she would be able to spend the summer with Skylark too – even though Bella would be riding her.

"We're filming up at the South Grange Estate over the next three weeks," Rob added. "So we can slot the riding scenes into filming, as and when they're perfected."

"Sounds good," Sarah said. "As long as we have enough time between the shoots to practice."

Rob grinned. "I'll arrange a suitable time in the next few weeks for the stunt riders to come over and trial the horses."

"Perfect," Sarah said. "Let's see... Bella, can you come to Sandy Lane tomorrow at, say, 10 o'clock? We can give you a try-out to see where you're at."

"Oh I don't need a try-out," Bella said quickly. "I know how to ride."

"Everyone at Sandy Lane has a try-out," Sarah

replied, firmly. "So I'll see you tomorrow."

Bella rolled her eyes, then wandered off towards the car.

"That's fine," Rob said, glancing at Sarah with a pained expression in his face. "So sorry about her." He spoke in a low voice. "She's just used to getting what she wants. I'll have the contracts sent over with her tomorrow."

Sarah nodded. "No problem, Rob."

A few minutes later, the car was reversing out of the drive. Bella, Miranda and Rob had left.

"Thank you, Jess," Nick said, squeezing her shoulder. "We might have lost the deal otherwise, so we really appreciate you doing this for us."

"That's all right." Jess fiddled awkwardly with Skylark's lead rope. "It's nothing."

"It's not nothing, Jess," Sarah said gently. "I know it'll be hard seeing the others training for Colcott and not being able to take part yourself. But this is a really great opportunity for you, too. Being able to ride side-saddle is a specialist skill."

Jess grinned. "I know. Thanks Sarah."

"And I'm sure Bella won't be so bad once she's settled in with the training," Sarah went on. "She's probably just nervous."

"Yeah, probably." Jess smiled weakly. She hoped that things would be all right with Bella, but a nagging suspicion told her that it wasn't going to be as easy as Sarah thought.

Chapter 3

A Bad Start

"I can't believe it." Tom roared with laughter. "You pushed Bella Ford into a puddle? *The* Bella Ford? What were you thinking, Jess?"

The regular riders were gathered in the tack room, discussing what had happened the day before. It was cosy inside the room, with its moth-eaten armchairs, faded but cheerful curtains, and tattered pony magazines scattered across the floor.

Jess laughed too. "I was only trying to help. But you should have seen the look on her face," Jess added, as Tom's face creased up. "It was priceless."

"So you're really going to learn to ride side-saddle?" Rosie said. "That's cool, Jess. I'd love to get the chance to do that."

"Yeah, I know," Jess agreed.

"So, tell us," Alex Hardy interrupted. "What's the famous Bella like?" He grinned sheepishly.

"Don't ask," Jess replied. "Besides, you'll meet her in a minute. She's coming for her try-out. But you should have heard what she said to me yesterday." Jess closed her eyes, enjoying the attention. "'You ridiculous girl... look at the state of me,'" she whined, imitating Bella's voice. She opened her eyes, and immediately noticed a strange look on Rosie's face.

"What's wrong, Rosie?"

Rosie cleared her throat and looked at the door.

Jess spun round to see Bella standing there. Jess felt her face flush red. "Oh... um... hi Bella..." she stuttered. "We've got Skylark tacked up, ready for you. I'll just come—"

But Jess didn't have a chance to finish her sentence, before Bella had disappeared out of the door. "Oh no." Jess put her head in her hands. "And I was going to try to get on with her!"

"Don't worry, Jess." Tom patted her on the back. "Just apologize to her later."

"Yeah, I guess so," Jess said glumly, though the thought of apologizing to Bella really did not appeal.

"She doesn't look all that bad, if you ask me." Alex grinned mischievously.

"Trust you to say that, Alex Hardy," Rosie observed, flicking him with a riding glove.

Jess hurried out of the tack room, and saw Bella on the other side of the yard with Skylark. She felt a twinge of jealousy as she watched Bella swing up into the saddle of her pony. Taking a deep breath, Jess made her way over to them, and stopped by Skylark's side to check the girth.

"Look, Bella, I'm sorry about that back there," Jess mumbled. "I know we didn't get off to a very good start, but can we put it behind us?"

But Bella seemed not to have heard or, if she had, she was ignoring the question.

"Can you get a cloth?" Bella said at last. "There's a patch of dirt on the saddle. I don't want it rubbing on my jodhs."

"Sure." Jess gritted her teeth as she dashed into the tack room, then back to Bella with a cloth.

Without a word of thanks, Bella grabbed the cloth, wiped the saddle, and threw the cloth at Jess.

"Hi there, Bella," Sarah called as she walked into the yard. "Good to see you've already mounted. Let's make our way to the outdoor school."

Jess followed on behind as Sarah led Bella and Skylark down the drive. At the bottom, Sarah opened the gate to the outdoor school and Bella walked Skylark through. Jess perched on the white railings at the edge to watch.

"Right," Sarah called across the school. "I know that you've done a little riding before, Bella, but we'll take it nice and slowly to start. Let's see what you can do." She walked over to Skylark and clipped the lunge rein onto the lunging cavesson onto Skylark's bridle. "Let's start at a walk."

Lightly, Sarah tapped Skylark with the lunging whip. "Concentrate on settling your seat into the deepest part of the saddle," she called. "Relax your lower back... That's good."

Jess squinted in the sun as she watched Skylark and Bella circle the school.

"Let your body flex with the movement," Sarah instructed. "Yes, that's right. Try not to tense your muscles, and you don't need to grip with your knees."

"Hey Jess," Tom said, as he joined Jess on the railings with Alex and Rosie.

"Hey guys." Jess greeted her friends. "Check this out – Sarah's taking her right back to basics."

"Still, she doesn't look too bad, does she?" Rosie said, as they all sat watching the training session going on in front of them.

Jess's eyes narrowed. Rosie was right. As much as Jess hated to admit it, Bella didn't look bad at all.

"Relax your back and seat muscles," Sarah called. "That's good! You're a natural, Bella."

Next, Sarah clicked them on into a canter.

"Skylark's doing pretty well, too," Tom said, nudging Jess.

Jess watched closely as Skylark and Bella circled the school. Of course it was better for Skylark that Bella could ride and yet Jess couldn't help feeling a little jealous at the thought of Skylark performing so well for someone else.

"Right, that's enough lunge work," Sarah said finally, as she started to arrange three poles in a row on the ground. "We'll try you over these."

Clicking Skylark on with her heels, Bella trotted her neatly over them.

"Good," Sarah said. "I'll add a couple more."

Bella trotted Skylark over the neat line. Her poise was perfect; she looked calm and Skylark trotted forward with rhythm and balance. Maintaining a light contact with the reins, Bella gently posted to the rise and fall of the trot.

"Now for a couple of jumps," Sarah called, erecting a set of cross-poles at the end of the row of trotting-poles. "Remember, it's important to let

Skylark do the work. Don't alter her balance by pushing her into the jump."

Bella nodded and, as she turned Skylark over the poles in a rising trot, her hips were bent in readiness. Skylark reached the end and they popped over the cross-poles with ease.

"Excellent." Sarah smiled.

"Well, she's obviously ridden before," Jess said to Rosie through gritted teeth.

The jumping exercise was over and now Bella was cantering Skylark around the school.

"OK, I think we've done enough for today," Sarah called out finally. "You've got all the basics very nicely. We'll begin side-saddle training next time."

Jess walked into the ring, intending to lead Skylark back to the yard.

"Traitor," she whispered into Skylark's neck, nuzzling her fondly.

"Let go, Jess. I can manage on my own." Bella frowned and tightened her reins.

Jess went to say something, but stopped herself

and let go. *Just let her get on with it*, Jess thought.

The other regulars had jumped down off the railings and were already following them up the drive. Rosie came to join Jess and gave her arm a friendly squeeze.

"That was a pretty good show, Bella," Tom said, smiling up at the teen star in admiration. "I'd ask you to join in with my jumping practices if you were going to be here full-time."

"Thanks." Bella flashed him a smile. "But I don't think the director would allow that."

"Trust Tom to play up to her," Rosie whispered.

Rosie and Jess stood back a bit as Bella and Skylark came into the yard. Alex rushed forward to help Bella as she dismounted.

"So, Bella, how long does it take to make a film?" Alex asked.

"Is it hard to learn your lines?" Tom continued.

"What's the director like?"

"Do you get to go to lots of film premieres?"

Bella flicked her long, glossy hair and laughed.

"So many questions!" she drawled. "Why don't you come to the set one day and take a look around? I could show you how it all works."

Alex gasped. "Er... that would be cool," he said, trying his best to sound unconcerned.

"That sounds awesome, Bella," said Tom.

"Let's say Wednesday. I'll let the movie crew know you're coming. Now, here's my car," Bella said, as the black Mercedes drove into the yard. "You don't mind sorting out Skylark, do you, Jess?" Bella flung Jess Skylark's reins without waiting for a reply.

Jess gritted her teeth again, and turned away.

"I think she's trying to wind you up, Jess," Rosie said, catching up with Jess as she led Skylark back to the stable. "It looks as though you've got a battle on your hands."

"Yeah." Jess frowned. "Well, she might be used to getting what she wants, but I'm not going to let her walk all over me."

Chapter 4

Rising Tensions

"See you guys later," Tom called, hopping onto his mountain bike.

It was a warm Wednesday morning and Jess and Rosie stood grooming their ponies in the yard. Alex and Tom were just about to cycle over to the film set to meet Bella and take a look around.

"Have fun with the film stars," Jess said, failing to disguise the sarcasm in her voice. "Make sure you're back in time to take your lessons."

"Don't nag, Jess. Of course I'll be back in time," Tom replied, as he and Alex cycled down the drive.

"Come on, Jess," Rosie said to her friend. "Bella Ford has caused enough problems for one week. Let's get these ponies tacked up and go out for that ride we've been promising ourselves."

"You're right. Where shall we go?" Jess asked.

"The beach," Rosie said decidedly.

Jess smiled and followed Rosie into the tack room to collect the saddles.

"Ready?" Jess said, after the girls had finished tacking up their ponies.

"You bet." Rosie tightened Midnight's girth and sprung up into the saddle.

"Come on, Skylark," Jess said, positioning herself carefully. Gently she nudged her pony forward to the back of the yard. Unlatching the gate, she held it open with her leg to let Rosie through. Soon the girls were out in the open fields.

Jess took a long, deep breath and put all thoughts about Tom, Alex, and Bella to the back of her mind. Pushing Skylark into a canter, she headed for the little hedge on the other side of the fields. As

Skylark's stride began to lengthen, the grass began to slip away beneath them, and Jess felt as though they were flying across the ground. After a few moments, she drew Skylark down to a trot and headed for the trees with Rosie.

As the two girls entered Larkfield Copse, they lost themselves in their riding. Skylark's coat shone like polished pewter as the sun beat down on their backs. Crossing the old coastal track, they emerged out into the open fields that led to the cliff tops. Skylark snorted excitedly, swishing her tail with a determined air. Jess nudged Skylark into a canter, crouching low in the saddle. Pounding across the springy turf, they seemed to be covering miles.

"Brilliant!" Jess looked at her watch as she drew Skylark back down to a trot and then a walk.

The scent of sea salt hung in the air as they reached the top of the cliff. Rosie slowed down to stop and Jess paused to look down onto the beach below. A shimmering silvery expanse of water stretched out in front of them.

"I'll follow you down," Jess called to Rosie.

Rosie nodded and, slowly, she began her descent to the beach. Jess followed suit.

The path wasn't steep, but Jess leaned back in the saddle to steady Skylark, and soon they were down on the sand. She looked across at Rosie and Midnight. The black thoroughbred's neck was arched, his hind legs tucked perfectly beneath him as he waited for Rosie to give the signal on the reins that would say he could go faster.

"Steady Midnight," Rosie crooned, as her horse jogged up and down on the spot. She turned to Jess and nodded.

Rosie squeezed her legs and fed her horse the reins. In no time at all she was galloping across the sands, with Jess and Skylark following close behind.

The two girls surged up the beach, the spray from the sea flying up in their faces. Out of breath but exhilarated, Jess drew Skylark down to a canter and then a trot. She turned to Rosie, her eyes alight with excitement. "That was amazing!" she breathed.

The two friends walked Skylark and Midnight back up the cliff path, across the scrubland and through the open fields. Jess had almost forgotten about the trip to the film set, until she neared the back gate of Sandy Lane and heard the sound of raised voices.

"You could have at least let me know. I'd have arranged for Sarah to take your lessons..." It was Nick, and he sounded angry. "You can't just go off when you feel like it, Tom. You've got commitments here. Who did you think would take your lessons?"

Jess jumped down from the back of Skylark and opened the back gate to the yard.

"I'm sorry, Nick," Tom said, as he shuffled his feet around in the gravel. "It won't happen again."

Jess and Rosie glanced at each other.

"Come on, Rosie," Jess said. "Let's clean up these horses and give the situation a chance to blow over."

Just then, Alex appeared from Puzzle's stable behind them. "All right, girls?"

"You're looking very pleased with yourself today,"

said Rosie, as she jumped down from Midnight.

"You would be too if you'd been with us." Alex grinned. "You should have seen the film set. It was something else."

"Oh yeah?" Jess said.

"Bella introduced us to everyone – even the director," Alex went on.

"Really?" Jess tried to sound uninterested, but she knew it wasn't working.

"Yes, really." Alex followed Jess into Skylark's stable where Jess began rubbing her pony down. "We also met the location manager: she's responsible for choosing where they film the scenes."

"And did you see any filming in action?" Jess asked, reluctantly.

"Yep!" Alex answered, proudly. "They were shooting on the lawns of the estate. It's so funny – there's even someone who checks that everything matches from scene to scene – if an actor's hair is messy in one scene and tidy in the next – that sort of thing. And you wouldn't believe it..."

"Try me," Jess muttered.

"Well, Bella has even got her own assistant – and a hairdresser too!" Alex replied.

"Sounds fabulous," Jess said, rolling her eyes, knowing she looked petty but unable to help herself. "What's the film actually about anyway?"

"Well, Bella is playing a Victorian orphan called Mary, who goes to live with her uncle in the country," Alex explained. "But her uncle turns out to be really cruel, and Bella – I mean Mary – tries to run away. That's when the riding scenes come in, I think."

Jess didn't know what to say, so she turned away.

"Why are you being so weird, Jess?" Alex frowned.

"Weird?" Jess spun back round, suddenly feeling angry. She'd heard enough about the film set and Bella Ford. "Didn't you see how Bella spoke to me yesterday?" she snapped at him. "I might as well have been her slave."

Jess took a deep breath, knowing that it wasn't just that. Deep down, she felt envious of the teen star. Jess had noticed how people seemed to drop everything to be around her. Bella had it all – long, glossy hair, big green eyes and, it seemed, everything she asked for. And to make matters worse, she wasn't even bad at riding.

"Bella causing more trouble?" Rosie said, appearing at the stable door next to Alex.

"Hmm... not really." Jess shrugged, but she didn't sound too convincing.

Bella had only arrived three days ago, and already the regulars at Sandy Lane were arguing in a way Jess had never known before.

Chapter 5

Side-saddle Training

"Right, so we're ready, are we?" Sarah said, perching on the water trough in the yard.

Bella stood by Skylark, and Jess by Storm Cloud. Three days had passed since the boys had visited the film set, and since then, there had been no more bad feeling. Things had started to settle down again at Sandy Lane.

Jess tried a smile in Bella's direction, but she abruptly turned away. *Why is she always so off with me?* Jess wondered. Sighing, she tickled Storm Cloud's nose. She felt both nervous and excited:

side-saddle training was about to begin, and she really didn't want to embarrass herself in front of Sarah or Bella.

Jess looked at the side-saddle on Storm Cloud's back. It didn't look all that different from a normal saddle, she thought, except that it had two pommels on it.

Sarah jumped up from where she was sitting and walked over to the two ponies. She checked both saddles, then ran a hand under each side.

"There needs to be at least two to three fingers clearance between the saddle and the pony," she explained to the girls. "They look all right, but I'll check again when you've both mounted." Sarah smiled. "I think we're ready to go."

The two girls led the ponies across the yard and Sarah opened the gate to the outdoor school.

"Right," Sarah said, walking into the middle of the arena. "Let me help you mount your ponies."

Sarah lifted Jess up into the saddle and she carefully settled herself in. It felt strange with both her legs dangling down the left-hand side.

Next, Sarah walked over to Bella and Skylark.

"No, not there... hold my foot here," Bella said with irritation, as Sarah went to give her a leg-up.

"You need to spring as I lift," Sarah instructed. "OK, we're ready to start," she announced, after checking that Bella was settled.

"So, how do we sit?" Bella said impatiently.

"Well, as you can see, the side-saddle is designed to be ridden on the left-hand side," Sarah explained. "Put your right leg over the upper pommel, and your left leg under the lower pommel – that acts as a brace. Your left foot goes into the stirrup. You should find it a firm seat because of the grip you get from the right leg. In fact, the only way you can really fall off is if you're jumping and your horse slips..."

Gingerly, Jess lifted her leg around the top pommel. It felt a bit weird, but it probably just took some getting used to.

"I don't like how this feels," Bella whined.

"Yes, it'll probably feel a little odd at first," Sarah

agreed. "But you'll soon get used to it... Try asking your ponies to go forward into a walk."

Jess released the pressure on the reins and, using her seat, urged Storm Cloud on.

"You'll need to do more work with your seat, Bella," Sarah called. "You can't rely on your leg aids when you ride side-saddle."

"I'm not relying on my leg aids," Bella argued.

Ignoring Bella, Sarah continued to instruct. "Don't sit back on your seat bones. If you sit straighter in the saddle, it will give you a better grip. Your weight needs to be on your right thigh rather than on your hips."

Jess nodded, starting to enjoy the rhythm.

"You can't give any leg aids on the right-hand side," Sarah went on. "So you might need one of these," she said, handing them both a long riding stick each. "As you know, I'm not a big fan of whips or crops of any shapes or sizes. So use it sparingly, just as an extra aid or for a nudge."

Jess winced as Bella gave Skylark a sharp rap. She

glanced at Sarah, but she had been looking the other way and hadn't noticed.

"Keep your right shoulder back, Jess," Sarah called, as Jess followed around the school on Storm Cloud. "That will keep you straight in the saddle... Yes, that's good."

Jess nodded, fixed in concentration. She was starting to get the hang of this.

"Try to keep your right toe pointing down, Bella," Sarah said, as Bella struggled with the stirrup. "You won't have such a good grip if the toe is pointing up as your leg is away from the saddle."

Bella scowled and Skylark got another rap.

"That's good, Jess..." Sarah said. "Bella – as long as you're relaxed, Skylark won't tense up. Now, let's try a trot. Remember, it's a sitting trot."

"Not my favourite." Jess was locked in concentration as she urged Storm Cloud forward, but soon she relaxed deep into the saddle. It was nearly impossible not to bump around and, as she looked across at Bella, she noticed that she was having just as much trouble.

Sarah called them to a halt. "Well done, girls. I think that's enough for today. What did you think?"

"Easy." Bella smirked. "I don't know what all the fuss is about."

Sarah raised an eyebrow. "And how about you, Jess? How did you find it?"

"Well, it was a bit uncomfortable at first, but I really started to enjoy it," Jess replied.

Sarah nodded, looking pleased. Then, slowing them down to a walk, she opened the gate and the girls turned their horses back up the drive.

When they reached the yard, Jess was relieved to see Bella's car already waiting for her.

"Here, let me take Skylark," Rosie said, appearing out of Midnight's stable. Bella handed Rosie the reins, and slid down from the saddle.

"See you tomorrow at ten, Bella," Sarah called.

"Yeah," Bella muttered, before climbing into the Mercedes and slamming the door shut.

"Jess! How did side-saddle training go?" Rosie

asked, as Jess climbed down from Storm Cloud.

"Well, it wasn't so bad," Jess replied.

"You were fantastic, Jess," Sarah said. "You took to it really well – definitely a natural. Do you know, I think you'd make a fine stunt rider one day."

Jess beamed. That was high praise indeed, especially coming from Sarah.

"Oh by the way, training tomorrow is going to be slightly different," Sarah added. "I'm going to ask Bella to train in costume. I want to check it won't interfere with her riding."

"Well, this is going to be interesting." Jess smiled.

"No moaning, Bella," Sarah said, placing a big pile of clothing on the bench in the tack room the following morning. "You're going to have to ride in this costume for the film, so you need to get used to practising in it."

Bella wrinkled up her nose. "It looks so horrible and moth-eaten," she said, picking through the strange fabrics. "Ugh!"

Sarah turned to Jess. "Jess, I'm afraid you'll just have to watch this part. I hope you don't mind."

Jess shook her head. "Course not." But secretly she did feel a bit envious of Bella. She'd have liked to try on a Victorian riding habit to see how it felt.

"What on earth is this?" Bella bent down and picked up a long, black apron-like garment.

"It's a skirt." Sarah laughed.

"How can you even begin to ride in that?" Jess shook her head in disbelief.

"I have no idea," Bella said, holding the skirt up against her. Jess realized it was the first time she'd ever seen Bella smile.

"It's not that bad," Sarah said. "At least you can wear your jodhs underneath, which is more than most Victorian women were able to do."

"You mean the Victorians all rode in things as tight as this?" Bella picked up a fitted black jacket from the chair. "I've worn a few strange costumes in my time, but nothing at all like this."

Sarah laughed. "Come on, your ponies are tacked

up and waiting. Put the costume on quickly, Bella, and let's get going."

As Bella gingerly slid a skirt on over her jodhpurs, Jess picked up a small top hat.

"What's this, Sarah?" Jess asked.

"It's the hat that Bella will have to wear in the actual shots," Sarah explained. "That's a good point, actually. There's no protection in it at all, so it's especially important that you ride with care on the day of filming, Bella."

"Not another lecture," Bella groaned.

"Not a lecture," Sarah said firmly. "But you do need to be aware of the risks. While we're practising, you'll ride in a hard hat."

Jess looked on as Bella twisted her skirt in place and pulled a white frilled shirt on over her vest top. Suddenly, Bella looked completely different – nothing like the untouchable movie star who had first arrived at the stables.

"You look great, Bella," Sarah said. "Now turn around and I'll do your hair for you."

"Careful," Bella warned. "My hairdresser doesn't like other people touching my hair."

"I just need to put it in a net," Sarah said patiently.

Bella grumbled as Sarah swept her long, dark hair up into a bun and pinned it back.

"There you go. All done." Sarah stood back to admire her handiwork.

"It's really tight," Bella moaned.

"I'm afraid that's just how they wore it," Sarah said, adjusting the net. "Right. I'm going out to check the saddles," she said, disappearing out through the tack room door.

Left alone together, Bella glanced at Jess. "How do I look?"

"Pretty... er... impressive," Jess said, not knowing what to say. Then, Bella gathered up her skirt and did a quick twirl.

Jess laughed. Was it just her, or was Bella beginning to lighten up a little?

"So... um... how's it compare to the other costumes you've worn?" Jess ventured.

"Hmm... well, the last movie I was in was set in the sixties, so I had to wear these awful bell-bottoms," Bella replied. "Then the year before that, I was in a pantomime and had to dress like a cat."

"A cat!" Jess laughed. She couldn't imagine Bella wearing anything that made her look silly.

"Yeah, I wore these big pink fluffy ears and had a long tail," Bella replied. "I looked ridiculous."

"I'd have loved to have seen that," Jess said. "What did all your friends think? I bet they're really envious of you, being a famous film star and all."

Jess looked at Bella expectantly, but there was a long pause, and Bella walked towards the door. "Hurry up," she snapped, her voice suddenly cold. "Sarah's waiting."

Jess picked up her riding hat and followed Bella outside. How confusing. What had she said to make Bella turn against her again?

Chapter 6

Missing Out

The stables were buzzing with excitement as the last-minute preparations for the Colcott Horse Show got underway. Bella was filming some early scenes with Skylark at South Grange, and Jess was taking the opportunity to catch up with her friends. She hated being apart from Skylark, and desperately needed to distract herself.

The Sandy Lane regulars had been coming and going at such different times over the last few days, Jess hadn't had a chance to see Rosie, let alone speak to her. Now, as she sat on the railings of the outdoor school, watching Tom take the last Colcott training session, she felt strangely out of it.

Jess watched as Rosie sailed over a jump on Midnight, and gave Alex a high-five as she trotted past. Jess felt a lump rise in her throat. She missed training with her friends.

"Well done, Rosie," Tom called across the school. "But try to give Midnight a wider sweep before the jump so that he can take a good look at it. Why don't you give it one more go?"

Jess smiled to herself. She even missed Tom's criticism. She'd never found practising as much fun as the actual shows, but now she realized how much she'd like to be up there on Skylark.

Rosie circled Midnight and positioned him at the first jump. Carefully, he popped over it. Landing gracefully, they cantered for the shark's teeth. As they reached the jump, Midnight rocked back on his hocks, and sprang over it as if it were alight. The black thoroughbred soared around the course, clearing jump after jump in steady succession.

"Much better, Rosie," Tom clapped as she drew to a halt. "I can't fault you on that."

Rosie beamed as she walked Midnight over to say hello to Jess. "Hey stranger!"

"You two have really come on," Jess said, hopping off the railings.

"Have we?" Rosie looked pleased.

"Yeah, definitely. I've missed you!" Jess said.

"Yeah, well if you will spend so much time with your new best friend Bella," Rosie teased.

"Bella?" Jess scoffed. "She's too busy and important to even bother talking to me." Jess felt a wave of loneliness wash over her, and she stared at her feet. "I hope I've done the right thing, Rosie," she said eventually. "Lending Skylark to someone else and not competing at Colcott. Hanging out with you guys over the summer is always the highlight of my year."

"Of course you have, Jess," Rosie said, giving her friend a gentle nudge. "Don't even think that you're missing out on anything here. Think of the opportunity you've been given – to learn side-saddle with Sarah! It's a fantastic chance."

Jess smiled. "I guess so," she said. "It's just hard, that's all. Bella is *so* cold towards me, and I miss you lot. I don't want you to forget about me!"

"Of course we won't," Rosie replied. "But you've done the right thing. And, you know, when Skylark becomes famous, you'll get to show off all your side-saddle skills to us."

"I guess," Jess said again, tracing an outline with her toe in the gravel.

"Oh Jess..." Rosie smiled. "You're only feeling like this because Colcott is days away and everyone's busy getting prepared for it."

"I know." Jess turned away, focusing her attention on Alex and Puzzle riding the course. Rosie was right. She was in a very lucky position. Why, then, did she have this funny feeling in the pit of her stomach, which refused to go away?

Chapter 7

And... Action!

As the days of summer passed, Bella started to spend more and more time down at Sandy Lane. Nearly three weeks had passed since their first side-saddle training session, but Jess still felt as if she hardly knew her. Apart from that slight thawing when they were looking at her costume, Bella had been as cold as ever. In fact, she seemed to be getting worse.

Sarah had announced yesterday that Bella was going to start filming the actual scenes. Although Jess felt disappointed that side-saddle training had come to an end so soon, she was relieved at the thought of having a break from the moody teen star.

As Jess led Storm Cloud out of her stable that morning, she saw Sarah leaning against the water trough, her head buried in a bundle of papers.

"Is that the film script?" Jess asked, walking over to join her.

Sarah nodded, flicking through the pages.

"So what do they want Bella to do?" Jess leaned over her shoulder. "Are the scenes difficult?"

"Not really," Sarah replied. "We're starting with the beach scene this afternoon. I think Bella is ready for it now."

Jess nodded. Bella and Sarah had been training down at the beach all week.

"Then there's a trickier cross-country scene next week," Sarah went on. "Bella's character, Mary, is chased by three footmen on horseback. This is the part in the plot where she's trying to escape from her uncle. The stunt riders are coming over tomorrow to try out their horses. It's quite a challenging scene to perfect. I just hope Bella is up to it."

Jess listened eagerly. "A chase scene! Sounds dramatic," she said.

Sarah smiled. "It should work very nicely. As long as Bella performs well. Now, I'm meeting Bella and the film crew at the beach in half an hour," Sarah went on. "Do you want to come? You could see how filming a stunt works."

"I'd love to," said Jess.

"CUT!" the director bellowed. "I've told you already, Bella. We need to see your face as you ride away. We want to see terror... pure terror as you gallop into the waves."

Jess stood in the sand, watching the shoot from behind a yellow rope. It was later that afternoon, and filming for the beach scene was in full swing. A small crowd of onlookers had gathered next to Jess.

Bella was already on her fourth take. Jess could see that she looked tired, and Skylark seemed to be getting more restless by the minute. *Acting is a lot harder than it looks like on screen,* Jess thought. *It can't be fun getting shouted at all the time.*

Jess looked at her phone – five o'clock already. The sun was low in the sky, and a pinkish glow lit up the surrounding vans and cameras. Looking across the beach, she noticed Sarah looking serious.

Suddenly, Jess realized how important it was that Bella got this right. It would reflect badly on Sandy Lane if they hadn't perfected the scene.

Jess looked forward again. The clapperboard snapped down and the cameras rolled forward on wooden planks as Bella rode Skylark into the waves. This time, Bella's cursory glance over her shoulder expressed a look of terror. Jess could see immediately that she had got it right. Skylark pranced forward and Bella released the reins. They cantered through the water and up the beach, the camera following in their wake.

"CUT!" the director shouted. Jess held her breath. "Wonderful," he called. "That's it for today... Well done team, that was just right."

As Bella cantered Skylark back to the cameras, the crowd of onlookers gave her a round of applause. She smiled as she dismounted and led Skylark over to the yellow rope.

"Bella! Over here!" A group of teenage girls in the crowd desperately tried to get Bella's attention. "Can we have your autograph?"

Beaming, Bella flicked her hair out of her eyes and laughed. "Of course."

Jess slipped under the rope and walked over to collect Skylark's reins. "I'll take him back, Bella," she said. "Well done, you were great!"

"Thanks," Bella mumbled, before turning back to pose for a selfie.

Jess watched, feeling pangs of envy as Bella played up to the camera, pouting and flicking her hair as if it were the most natural thing in the world.

Leading Skylark away, Jess sighed. Nobody had even noticed her and Skylark leave. They were all too busy congratulating Bella on her star performance. Even Sarah was deep in conversation, discussing the next scene with the director.

Jess kissed Skylark's neck fondly. "You were the real star, Skylark," she whispered in her pony's ear. "Nobody else might say it, but you stole the show."

Chapter 8

The Colcott Show

The morning of the Colcott Show dawned bright and clear. As everyone dashed around the yard gathering body brushes, curry combs and hoof oil, Jess stood back and looked on, feeling strangely detatched from everything.

"Hey Jess!" Rosie called as she hurried past with Midnight's bridle slung over her shoulder.

"Rosie! I—" But the rest of Jess's sentence was cut short as Rosie called across the yard for Alex to hurry up with the hoof oil.

"Sorry, what was that, Jess?" Rosie called back.

"I just wanted to wish you lots of luck." Jess bit her lip, feeling sad she couldn't take part. "I'll be thinking of you."

A big grin spread across Rosie's face. "Thanks Jess." She gave her friend a quick hug. "We'll miss you!" Then she hurried off across the yard.

"You OK, Jess?" Sarah came up behind her, holding Zoe in her arms.

"I guess so." Jess sighed. Sarah always seemed to be able to read her thoughts.

"You know, I really do appreciate all the time you're putting in here," Sarah said, shifting Zoe on to her hip so she could ruffle Jess's hair. "I know there's no more side-saddle training now, but I'm still counting on your help with Bella's run-through at the set this afternoon. It's for the last scene – the cross-country chase. You know, Bella always seems more relaxed when you're around."

"She does?" Jess almost choked. "Why on earth would she be more relaxed around me?"

Sarah smiled. "I think she likes you, Jess."

Jess frowned. "Well, if she does, she's got a funny way of showing it."

Sarah gave Jess's arm a squeeze. "Now, the box is coming to collect the horses at nine to take them to the film set. I'll come and help once Zoe's babysitter arrives. Do you mind helping with the horses?"

"Sure thing," Jess replied.

As Sarah walked back up to the cottage with Zoe, Jess spotted Nick emerging from the tack room.

"Right, folks, are we nearly ready to go?" he called. He bent down and lifted a saddle onto Whispering Silver's back, and, tightening the girth, swung up onto her back.

A murmur of excitement spread across the yard, as the Colcott competitors gathered with their ponies. It was a Sandy Lane tradition for all of the competitors to ride over to the show together.

Among the crowd was Tom, mounted on his horse, Horton Chancellor. Behind him, Alex sat adjusting his seat on Puzzle, and just swinging up onto Midnight was Rosie.

"Good luck guys," Jess called out. "Have fun!" She waved as the horses and riders clattered down the drive, trying to ignore the knot in her stomach as they all disappeared around the corner.

But Jess didn't have much time to dwell on it, before the horsebox arrived to collect the horses. With the help of the driver, she began to load Hector, Minstrel, Napoleon and Skylark into the box.

"Thanks, Jess!" Sarah said brightly, just as Jess had finished settling the last horse down. "The babysitter's all set now." She climbed into the Land Rover, and started up the engine. "Hop in. We'll follow the box down to the set."

Three bends and another two roads later, Jess and Sarah were pulling up at the film set at South Grange. As they climbed out of the Land Rover, a woman in jeans appeared with a set of headphones around her neck.

"Hi Sarah," the woman said. "Thanks for getting here on time. We're all ready for the cross-country run-through."

"Ah great," Sarah replied. "Linda – this is Jess. She's helping out. Jess – this is Linda, the assistant director. She's taking the run-through today."

"Nice to meet you, Jess!" Linda said, shaking her hand. "Why don't you follow me? The horses are just being prepared."

Linda led Sarah and Jess across a large lawn to the edge of the estate. There, Jess looked out across a huge meadow, several acres in length. On the far side, there was a coppice of oak trees. On the other, there was a stream with a hedge behind it. In the distance, Jess saw Napoleon, Hector and Minstrel being warmed up by three men riding bareback. The men were dressed in black jackets and long leather boots. *They must be the stunt riders,* she thought, watching them with fascination. They looked so skilled and athletic.

"Ugh! This stupid skirt..." Jess recognized Bella's voice immediately. She spun around to see her squirming about in Skylark's saddle, pulling angrily at her long skirt.

"Listen up," Linda announced. "I'm just going to give you all a brief run-through of the scene."

Jess listened carefully as Linda began to explain the scene: the chase was going to be taken from one length of the meadow to the other, where Bella would finally be cornered by the stream. Skylark and Bella would be given a head start before the other stunt riders gave chase. In the middle of the meadow, Bella was to look back over her shoulder for the first time. Then, when she was three-quarters of the way across the field, she was to look back a second time. Finally, when she was caught, she was to look back one last time.

Jess thought it sounded simple enough, and settled down on the fence to watch the proceedings.

"OK, is everyone ready?" Linda glanced at Sarah. "I'll take a step back for now and leave you to work out the technicalities. Bella – you need to join the other riders."

Bella nudged Skylark forward, still wriggling about on the saddle.

She seems anxious, Jess thought to herself.

"Hey, Bella," she called out. "Good luck!"

Bella looked back at Jess and, for a moment, Jess thought she saw her smile.

Sarah stood with a stick in her hand, mapping out the scene on the grass. "Be careful when you reach the hedge, everyone," she warned. "It's pretty boggy over by the stream. OK Bella, off you go."

Bella nudged Skylark into a trot, then a canter. But something seemed wrong, and Bella's balance looked off.

"Stop!" Sarah shouted.

"What did I do wrong?" Bella slowed Skylark down to a halt.

"Remember what I taught you in the outdoor school? The weight has to be on your right thigh rather than your hips. You need to look like an accomplished horsewoman."

Bella frowned.

"Again," said Sarah.

Bella turned back to the start of the field and

readied herself once more. Jess's eyes narrowed as she watched the second prompt. Bella's weight was still in the wrong place, but Sarah didn't stop her this time. Bella turned awkwardly in the saddle and looked over her shoulder as the riders gave chase.

Sarah called the group to a stop, and shook her head. "No, no. We haven't got it right yet." She turned around and, waving in Jess's direction, called for her to come over.

"Me?" Jess shouted, her heart thudding in her chest. She jumped down off the wooden fencing and ran across the grass towards the group.

"Bella, can you jump down off Skylark for a moment and let Jess have a go?" Sarah said, looking up at the actor. "I just want to show the chase riders what I mean."

Jess saw a flicker of anger pass across Bella's face, and she scowled down at Jess. "I can do the scene perfectly well," Bella muttered.

"You haven't got it quite right, yet." Sarah stood firm. "Let Jess take the saddle."

Jess looked at Sarah, feeling awkward. She didn't want to upset Bella, but she had promised to help Sarah. Finally, after a long pause, Bella reluctantly jumped down.

Jess accepted Sarah's leg-up and settled herself into Skylark's saddle. It just felt so natural being back on her pony, and Jess had been longing for a moment like this for weeks. She didn't care that everyone was watching her – she was just savouring every second with Skylark.

"Right, let's go," said Sarah, walking back off across the grass. "You know what Linda wants from the scene, don't you Jess?"

Jess nodded, feeling Bella's angry gaze burning into her back. Waiting for the signal, she pushed Skylark into a canter, making sure that her weight was forward and that she was sitting straight in the saddle. A rush of energy flooded through her. Skylark responded to the gentle squeeze from Jess's legs and Jess felt a little bubble of excitement as she heard the pounding hooves of the other riders on their way. *One... two... three...* Jess looked back over her shoulder as she cantered. Now she was at the halfway point... at the three-quarter point... the chase riders were gaining on her all the time, and all at once she was cornered by the hedge. Satisfied, she drew Skylark to a halt, and trotted her back towards Sarah.

"Perfect," Sarah cried, her eyes sparkling. "Did you see how it was done, Bella?"

Bella's eyes narrowed and she snatched the reins out of Jess's hands. "Sure."

Trying her best to be helpful, Jess jumped off Skylark and put out her hands to give Bella a leg-up into the saddle.

"Oops, sorry, Jess," Bella said, catching Jess's chin with her boot as she sat down.

"That's OK." Jess's eyes smarted and she rubbed her chin. *She kicked me on purpose,* Jess thought, making her way back to the fence.

"Let's try again Bella," Jess heard Sarah call. Climbing back onto the fence, Jess settled down at a safe distance, wondering what on earth she had done to make Bella hate her so much.

"What a long day." Sarah sighed, shifting gears in the Land Rover. She and Jess were driving back to the stables, having spent all afternoon at the film set. "Thanks for your help today, Jess. I know it's difficult for you."

Jess nodded, absently staring out of the window.

"And I know Bella is hard work. She doesn't make it easy for people to like her," Sarah went on. "But I really think, underneath all the bravado, she's just a bit insecure."

Jess sighed. "Hmm, I don't know, Sarah..." How could Bella be insecure when she looked and acted the way she did? Jess couldn't believe it.

"Anyway, forget about it now," Sarah said. "Let's see how the others got on at Colcott. I bet they're dying to tell us all about it!"

Colcott! Jess realized with a jolt that she'd been so tied up with the film, she hadn't even thought about how they'd all done at the show.

As the Land Rover drew to a halt, Jess leaped out into the yard to hear the sound of excited voices. Dozens of riders streamed across the yard; some were watering the ponies while others rubbed down their mounts. Jess found Rosie in Midnight's stable, filling up his water trough.

"So how did you do?" Jess said excitedly.

"Well..." Rosie's eyes lit up. "We won – Midnight and I – we won the Open Jumping!"

"Really?" Jess answered. "But that's brilliant!"

"We beat Tom and Chancey." Rosie could hardly contain her excitement. "And then that girl, Jessica March, who's been tipped for the Junior Olympic team. She only got second place. We went clear in 56 seconds; Tom and Chancey knocked two jumps..." The words tripped off Rosie's tongue.

"That's great, Rosie." Jess gave her friend a hug. She felt pleased for Rosie, but still sad to have missed all the excitement.

"So tell me about your afternoon," Rosie said,

walking out of the stable with Jess.

"Oh, you know, it was all right," Jess said glumly. "Bella was playing up as usual." What she really wanted to say was that she'd had a miserable afternoon, Bella had kicked her on purpose and given her the cold shoulder all day.

"So have you heard how we all did?" Nick came up behind Jess and Rosie, beaming with pride. "Two firsts – in the Novice and the Open, five seconds and three fifths. Oh and a little silver trophy for Rosie – nice to think that it's being returned to the Sandy Lane for safe keeping, eh?"

Jess smiled. "It's great! I'm so proud of you, Rosie."

At that moment there was the sound of a motor and a horsebox turned up the drive. The ramp was lowered and, one by one, Hector, Minstrel, Napoleon and Skylark were led out.

Skylark gave a little whinny when she saw Jess, and Jess rushed forward to grab her lead-rope.

"Come up to the cottage for the celebrations after you've finished with Skylark," Nick said. "I'm going up now to get everything ready."

Jess nodded and led Skylark to the side of the yard to give her a quick rub-down.

As the yard fell quiet, Jess stood with her pony nose-to-nose.

"Listen up, girl," she whispered. "Tomorrow's a big day – your last one at the set. Show them what you're capable of, and make me proud!"

Chapter 9

The Final Scene

"Come on, Jess. Up you get... You're going to be late," Jess's mother shouted up the stairs.

"Urgh," Jess groaned and rolled over, burying her face in the pillow. It had been a late night – the Colcott celebrations had gone on past eleven and she felt exhausted.

Yawning, Jess sat up in bed and threw off her duvet. She couldn't lie in bed all morning. It was the last day of filming and Skylark's big day! She had to make sure her pony was looking immaculate.

"I'll be down in a sec," Jess yelled.

She dragged a comb through her hair and pulled on her jodhs. Then she ran down the stairs and into the kitchen to grab a quick breakfast.

Less than ten minutes later, Jess was on her bike and making her way to the stables. She pedalled down Ash Hill and past the old tannery, until at last she turned into Sandy Lane.

"Morning guys!" Jess called, spotting Alex and Tom in the yard.

"Hi Jess," they grunted, both sounding a little worse for wear.

Jess hurried into the tack room to grab a head-collar from the rack, then headed straight into Skylark's stable.

"Now, you've got to look your absolute best today," Jess said, leading the little pony out into the yard. She grabbed a bucket and began Skylark's beauty routine. First, she washed her tail, then she used a curry comb to remove all the loose hairs from Skylark's coat. With firm, flicking motions, she followed on with a dandy brush, then finally, she buffed Skylark from head to toe with a body brush.

Jess stood back and admired her handiwork. Skylark's coat shone like shimmering clouds of grey, and her mane looked soft and silky.

"Perfect." Jess smiled, turning as she heard the sound of bike wheels screeching to a halt. It was Rosie jumping off her bike.

"Wow, doesn't she look great?" Rosie grinned.

"Well, I should think so too," Jess said. "A film star in the making!"

"So what's the plan for today?' Rosie asked.

"The horses are being picked up any minute now to be taken to the set." Jess glanced at her phone. "Sarah's taking the Land Rover for anyone who wants to go over and watch."

"Count me in," said Rosie.

Jess grinned. "I think Alex and Tom are coming too. Nick's staying behind to watch Zoe."

Jess and Rosie turned to see the horsebox rattle into the yard. The driver turned off the engine and jumped out of the cab, then began loading Hector,

Napoleon, Minstrel and Skylark into the box.

Then Alex, Tom, Rosie and Jess squeezed into the back of the Land Rover and, with Sarah at the wheel, the excitable group bumped down the lane towards the film set.

As they pulled up in the driveway to South Grange, Jess was the first to clamber out. The area was bustling with activity: there were runners carrying props, sound assistants with microphones on long leads, and camera operators fussing around their equipment.

Making her way over to the horsebox, Jess helped the driver unload the horses, and took hold of Skylark's reins. Skylark looked out over the meadow, alert and interested. Her neck was crested, and her nostrils quivered as she caught the scent of something on the wind.

"All right, girl, keep calm," Jess said as she patted her pony's neck and led her into the meadow.

Out of the corner of her eye, Jess spotted Bella. A group had gathered around her, including Tom and

Alex. Jess glanced at Rosie and rolled her eyes.

"I know – pathetic, aren't they?" Rosie whispered.

Jess took a deep breath and led Skylark forward, pleased to see the admiring glances from the growing crowd of onlookers. There were lots of people there – even reporters from the local press. Nervously, she walked over to where Bella was standing, and handed her Skylark's reins.

"Here you go, Bella," Jess said. "Good luck with the scene."

Bella snatched the reins and glared at Jess. "Thanks," she snapped. "Oh, and by the way – I know you think it should be you up there on Skylark instead of me. Well, Miss Perfect, I'll show you."

Jess's mouth fell open in surprise. "I– I– I don't think that at all, Bella," she stammered. *Is that what she really thinks of me?* Jess thought, shocked by her vicious words. How could Bella think Jess was perfect, when *she* was the one in the spotlight?

Bella turned away. Sweeping her long black skirt and petticoat up around her knees, she sprang up awkwardly into the saddle. Then she jerked Skylark round into a walk. Skylark hesitated and let out a little kick from her off-hind leg – obviously surprised by Bella's force.

Jess looked around to see if Sarah had noticed, but Sarah was deep in conversation with the director. Skylark moved forward at a collected canter and she and Bella circled the field.

"She looks good up there, doesn't she?" Alex said, as he and Tom came over to join Jess.

"She can't do anything wrong in your eyes," Jess retorted, suddenly feeling angry and confused.

"All right, take it easy." Tom raised his eyebrows.

"Skylark looks wonderful," Rosie said, joining the other regulars.

"Thanks Rosie." Jess tried to smile, but her eyes were fixed firmly on her pony as she cantered around the field. At the furthest end of the meadow, the chase riders circled their horses.

At last, everybody was ready. The director raised his arms and the cameras rolled. Bella sat on Skylark waiting for the signal to start.

And... ACTION! The clapperboard came down and Bella and Skylark were cantering across the field. Jess counted the timing silently in her head. And now the other riders were flying after them. Napoleon, Hector and Minstrel gave chase across the field.

Jess held her breath. Skylark and Bella were going pretty fast – so fast that Bella had missed her cue for looking around. The collected canter was now a full blown gallop. *What's she playing at?* Jess thought. She watched, dumbfounded, as Bella urged the reins up Skylark's neck. *Are they getting even faster?* Jess opened her mouth to shout, but closed it again. They were out of control!

Jess felt a sense of rising panic. *This isn't how we practised it in the run-through.*

The chase riders galloped faster and faster, but they weren't making any in-roads on Bella and Skylark. Jess felt giddy as she watched what was going on in front of her.

"Slow down..." she begged under her breath. "Slow down, Bella."

"What on earth?" Sarah appeared next to Jess, her face as white as a sheet. "There's no protection in that hat she's wearing... And she's going to come off at this rate."

"Cut... Cut!" the director cried out, as the horses neared the end of the meadow. He raised his hands in the air in frustration.

"Slow down," Jess willed, her eyes narrowing. If Bella didn't stop now they'd be in the hedge. Jess's heart was in her mouth. Surely Bella wasn't going to try to take Skylark over it? They'd never jumped side-saddle before, and who knew what was on the other side...

As the hedge loomed nearer and nearer, pony and rider raced faster and faster. Jess felt her breath catch in her throat. Skylark's neck was lathered with sweat. For a moment, it looked as though they were going to stop, but then Bella gathered up the reins and pushed Skylark onward. The little pony hesitated for a moment – as if she couldn't believe what was being asked of her. Then, bravely, she raised herself back onto her hocks and threw herself forward.

Jess's heart was in her mouth. "She's too near... she's not going to clear it..." she muttered, half covering her eyes. She could hardly bear to watch as Skylark reached forward for the leap. The pony's back legs slipped and gave way beneath her. As she lost the momentum to throw herself over the hedge, she went crashing through the top of it. There was a sickening crunch as the pony fell to the ground. Bella was thrown clear and lay in a heap on a grassy mound nearby.

"Noooooooo!" Jess cried, unable to believe the scene that had panned out in front of her. She stood, rooted to the spot, as she waited for a sign of movement from the other side of the hedge... But there was nothing.

"Get up, Skylark... get up!" Jess pleaded. Her mouth felt dry and she couldn't speak. For a moment, time seemed to stand still.

Then, she heard a loud scream. It was a while before she realized it was coming from her own mouth. There was a flash of blue and two medics ran past her. "Skylark..." Jess screamed, jumping up to follow them. "Skylark! Get up!"

Chapter 10

A Nasty Fall

Jess sprinted across the grass, her knees almost buckling as she neared the scene of the accident. As she reached the hedge, she threw heself down beside Skylark, who lay still on the ground. The little pony blinked, breathing heavily through her nostrils.

"It's going to be all right, Skylark." Jess wiped her sleeve across her teary face. "I'm here." She looked across to Bella, where a team of medics were crouched around her.

"She might just be winded," Sarah called out breathlessly, as she arrived with Rosie close behind.

"Give her a moment to try to get up." She turned to Rosie. "Call Nick," she said, pulling out a mobile phone from her puffer jacket. "Get him to send the vet here."

Jess looked up in panic. If Sarah wanted the vet to come out, it was pretty serious.

"Skylark... Skylark, please get up!" she whispered, bending her face level with her pony's. But Skylark did not move.

The sound of screeching sirens sounded in the distance, and Jess looked over at the crowd that had gathered around Bella. *What on earth was she thinking? She could have been killed!*

Jess turned back to her pony. "Skylark, my beauty," she breathed. "Please get up."

And then, as if somehow the pony had understood her owner, she let out a deep breath and slowly but surely clambered to her feet.

"Skylark!" Jess flung her arms around her pony's neck. But the injured mare flinched back, and Jess could see in an instant the pain in her eyes. Skylark held one of her hind legs from the ground, spreading the weight evenly around the other legs.

"Well, at least she's standing," Sarah said slowly. "But until the vet arrives, we won't know what damage she's done."

Breathlessly Rosie returned with Sarah's mobile in her hand. "I called Nick. The vet's on her way."

Jess looked at Sarah pleadingly. "She's going to be OK, isn't she, Sarah?"

Sarah ran a hand down Skylark's leg.

"Let's hope so," she replied. "There's heat, but we need to wait and see what the vet says." She laid a hand on Jess's shoulder. "I'm sure she won't be long. We just have to wait."

It could only have been ten minutes before the vet's horsebox was careering across the field. But to Jess, it felt like an eternity.

Stepping aside to give the vet space, Jess watched as the vet examined Skylark, expertly running her hand up and down the leg. Finally, the vet straightened up and began to speak.

"It's bad, but I'm not sure how bad." She looked at Sarah. "I'm going to have to get her back to the horse surgery. Until I take X-rays, I won't know what the damage is."

"But... isn't she well enough to come back with us?" Jess said. "We'll make her comfortable there..."

Sarah laid a hand on Jess's shoulder. "The vet knows what's best, Jess."

"Then I want to go with her," Jess said.

"I know you're worried." The vet looked at Jess kindly. "But I need to keep an eye on her tonight. She'll be in safe hands."

"But..."

"No buts, Jess," Sarah insisted.

Jess nodded, all the fight knocked out of her.

The vet ran to her trailer and returned with a big white bandage.

"It's an immobiliser for her leg," Sarah explained to Jess. "To keep everything in place."

Jess nodded, all the time rubbing gentle circles on Skylark's neck. She glanced across at Bella, who was being lifted onto a stretcher and into the ambulance. Suddenly, everything felt just too much, and Jess broke down in tears.

"It's going to be all right, Jess." Rosie gently put her arm around her friend's shoulder, as the vet led Skylark slowly up the ramp into the box.

"Come on, Jess." Sarah smiled reassuringly. "There's nothing more that we can do here. We'll just have to go back to Sandy Lane and wait there for any news."

Chapter 11

The Diagnosis

"Why hasn't the vet called?" Jess groaned. "She said she'd call as soon as she knew anything."

"It's only been a couple of hours, Jess," Nick said calmly. "She has to examine her thoroughly, do the X–rays, examine them..."

Sarah had rung Jess's mother, who was keen to have Jess home after the accident. But Jess knew that the stables would be the first place to hear news of Skylark, so that was where she wanted to be. Now, as she sat in the kitchen of the cottage with Nick and Sarah, she chewed on her fingernails anxiously.

"I wish we'd had nothing to do with this movie," Jess mumbled, picking at her fingernail. "What was I thinking, loaning Skylark out to Bella? I should have known."

She looked at Nick and Sarah and immediately felt guilty for what she was saying. They were blaming themselves enough as it was.

"It's not your fault, Jess," Sarah said quietly.

"No one could have known that this would happen," Nick added.

"But don't you see?" Jess sniffed. "If I hadn't ridden Skylark at the film set yesterday, Bella might not have felt the need to out do me. She might not have pushed herself that one step further."

"I think there's more to it than that," said Sarah. "Besides, you were just doing what I asked you to do. You've got to stop going over it again and again." Sarah stroked Jess's hair.

"I think we should phone Rob Fraser," Nick suggested. "See if there's any news of Bella."

Sarah nodded, walking out into the hallway with

the phone. Then she turned to face Nick and Jess as she dialled.

"Yes, hello... Rob? It's Sarah... Sarah Brooks. I was just phoning for news of Bella."

There was a pause, and Jess couldn't tell from Sarah's expression whether it was good or bad.

"Yes, I see, so she should be all right then?" Sarah smiled with relief. "No, there's no news on the pony yet... All right, yes, we'll keep you posted." With a small nod, Sarah put down the phone.

"Well?" Nick stood up from his chair.

"It looks as though she's going to be all right." Sarah smiled. "Apart from a broken leg, that is."

"A broken leg!" Jess gasped.

"Yes." Sarah nodded. "She suffered concussion, but she's come round. They want to keep her in overnight for observation..."

But Sarah stopped short suddenly, as they heard the sound of a horsebox rumbling up in the yard.

Jess's face darkened. "Skylark!"

"Jess..." Gently, Nick laid a hand on her shoulder

and gave it a squeeze. "Try not to worry."

Jess rushed out of the door and down into the yard, just as the vet was climbing down from the driver's seat.

"I couldn't get through on the phone so I thought I'd just bring her over," the vet said. "It's not as bad as I'd thought."

"Oh thank goodness... thank goodness for that," Jess breathed, as Nick and Sarah arrived behind her.

"It's not all good news though," the vet went on. "Skylark hasn't broken any bones but she obviously took a very nasty fall. She's torn a ligament. They can be notoriously difficult to heal, so she'll have a long recovery period ahead of her. But with the right treatment, she should make a full recovery."

"Oh Skylark..." Jess murmured, welling up with tears. "A-as long as she's going to be all right."

The vet looked sympathetically at Jess, then she turned to Nick. "We ought to unload her right away. She's tranquilized."

Jess followed Nick as he walked over to the

horsebox and let down the ramp. Then, anxiously, she peered inside. It took time for her eyes to adjust to the gloom, but she could just make out a pair of dull eyes looking back at her.

"She's not going to be herself for a few days," the vet said, as Jess climbed into the horsebox and untied the lead-rope. Gently, with Nick's help, she led Skylark down the ramp.

"She'll start to feel the real pain tomorrow," the vet explained. "Why don't you take her off to her stable and settle her in?" she said to Jess. "I'm going to need to talk to Nick about her treatment."

Jess nodded numbly and carefully led Skylark to her stable.

"I'll be back in a second," Jess murmured, as she hurried out to prepare Skylark a bran mash.

Pouring water onto the bran, Jess thought about what the vet had said. If time was what was needed to make Skylark better, then time was exactly what she would have. Jess would be there every step of the way.

Rushing back into Skylark's stable, Jess put the bucket of mash down on the floor. But the pony took one sniff at the offering and turned away.

"I know you're not hungry, girl." Jess stroked the injured mare. "But you've got to eat something."

Skylark didn't move, and her dull eyes gazed straight ahead. Jess looked at the injured leg in its long bandage, stretching from the fetlock to just above the knee joint.

"I'm going to stay with you night and day, Skylark," she soothed. "Whatever it takes."

"Jess..." Sarah's worried face appeared over the stable door. "I think it's time for you to go home, now. Skylark's going to need her space tonight."

"But she needs me around," Jess pleaded.

Sarah shook her head. "If you want to do the best thing by her, Jess, you'll let her have some time to herself to come to terms with the injury."

Jess nodded. She knew Sarah was right, however hard it would be to drag herself away.

"Now, come on," Sarah said kindly. "That was

your mother on the phone. I've said I'll drop you home now."

Jess nodded and, giving Skylark a pat on the forehead, she turned to leave the stable. As she bolted the door behind her, she took one last glance at the little mare. Her head was hung low, her eyes were dull and listless and her coat was matted with sweat. The spark seemed to have gone completely from her beloved pony. Would she ever get it back?

Chapter 12

A Proposal

"I'll give you a lift to the stables if you like," Jess's mother said, as her daughter made her way down the stairs the next morning. "You look exhausted."

Jess managed a weak smile. Her mother was right – she hadn't slept a wink last night. "Thanks Mum," she mumbled.

A short car ride later, and Jess was being dropped off at the bottom of Sandy Lane. It was still early and all was quiet as she walked into the yard. Hurrying over to Skylark's stable, she peered in to see the little mare lying in the straw.

"She didn't have too bad a night." Nick came up behind Jess and opened the door of the stable. "But I need to give her a shot of painkillers now. You might not want to watch this bit."

Jess swallowed hard. "No, I want to be with her," she said, as Nick began preparing Skylark's shot. Wincing as the injection was given, Jess gave Skylark a gentle rub on the nose, before walking out into the yard to get her some water.

Just then, she heard the sound of voices near the back gate. It was too early for lessons, and the stables were otherwise empty. Curious, Jess waited in the corner by the water trough. Then she saw Rob Fraser and Sarah walking up the drive. *What is Rob doing here?* she thought, hanging back to listen.

"So what do you think?" Rob was saying.

"Well, I don't know, Rob," Sarah replied. "I think Jess has taken a bit of a knock after everything that's happened with Skylark."

Jess was confused. *What were they talking about?* Sheepishly, she stepped forward.

"Ah Jess, there you are," Sarah called, beckoning her over. "Rob's got something to ask you."

Jess swallowed hard. She felt upset just seeing Rob. She knew it wasn't his fault, but she couldn't help thinking that if he hadn't shown up at Sandy Lane, none of this would ever have happened.

"The specialist has said that it will take three months – at least – before Bella is fully recovered," Rob started, looking at Jess.

Jess looked away. "Poor Bella," she mumbled. She felt sorry for her – but she still couldn't forgive her for what had happened to Skylark.

"Everything's been scheduled down to the last minute for the shoot," he went on. "So..." He took a deep breath. "We were wondering whether you'd take Bella's place for the last riding scene."

"Take Bella's place?" Jess couldn't believe what she was hearing.

Rob nodded. "At least then we'd have this last scene. And the digital team would edit the movie to make you look like Bella. It would be a real help,"

Rob said. "We can't see any way around this other than putting the entire movie on hold. And that could cause a whole heap of problems. In the worst case scenario, our movie distributor might end up scrapping it altogether."

"You've been watching all the scenes as Bella has been learning them," Sarah added, tentatively. "You could do them standing on your head."

Jess stared at the ground. She knew she should be excited by what Rob was offering, but the fact was, Skylark was seriously injured and it was all Bella's fault. She didn't want anything more to do with the film. It just felt too much – going back to the meadow where Skylark had fallen. She would relive the accident all over again. Even thinking about it was making her feel dizzy.

"I know you don't want to leave Skylark," Sarah said, "but she's in safe hands here. You can ride Storm Cloud for the shoot. She's a similar size and colour to Skylark."

Jess looked up at Sarah, then Rob, who smiled at

her pleadingly. "Well I don't know..." she said.

"You're exactly the same age as Bella," Rob added earnestly. "You're a little taller, but you'd never be able to tell that on horseback."

"If you're not feeling up to it, you don't have to agree," Sarah stressed. "It's been a really difficult time for you, I know."

Jess didn't know what to say. It made sense, of course. She knew the scenes like the back of her hand. But how could she even think about leaving Skylark on her own at this critical time? And to ride Storm Cloud on the film set instead? It felt like a complete betrayal.

"It would only be for a couple of days and I know that Rosie would take good care of Skylark for you," Sarah said, biting on her lip.

Jess hesitated. It suddenly dawned on her that Sarah needed her to do this... If the film was called off because of Bella's stunt riding accident, Sandy Lane's reputation would suffer. Sarah needed Jess to help put things to right. Sighing, Jess looked at the ground and fidgeted with her zip. "All right," she said. "I'll do it."

Rob clapped his hands together. "That's great news, Jess. I know everyone working on the movie will be really happy to hear that you're onboard. I can't thank you enough." Rob glanced at Sarah. "How long are you going to need to get her ready? We're only scheduled to be at South Grange for two more days.

"Two more days will be plenty," Sarah said firmly. "We'll practise this afternoon and be ready to shoot tomorrow. That sounds about right, doesn't it, Jess?"

Jess gulped. "Sure."

"I won't forget this, Jess," Rob added. "I mean it."

Chapter 13

Facing Fears

Jess sat on Storm Cloud at the side of the meadow, waiting for the director to give the word to start. It had been late by the time she'd finished practising yesterday, but finally it had all seemed to come together. She took a deep breath. Could it have been only a couple of days since she'd stood here, watching Skylark's accident unfold? She tried to shake off the painful memory.

Jess looked down at her costume, feeling the butterflies gather in the pit of her stomach. Her whole body felt hot and uncomfortable. When she'd watched Bella putting on the costume a few weeks ago, she'd felt envious. Now, she couldn't wait to take it off.

"Easy, Storm Cloud," Jess murmured. She reached down to pat the neck of the little pony and twisted her long, black skirt in the side-saddle.

"Good luck, Jess," Tom called, as he came over to her to check the girth one more time. "You look a million dollars!"

Jess laughed, trying to ignore the pangs of anxiety in her chest. She looked over at the fence, and saw Rosie and Alex waving at her. Even her mum had taken the day off work, and had come along to support her. "I'm pretty nervous," she said.

"You'll be great." Tom grinned and patted Storm Cloud's neck. "Just imagine you're into the jump-off at the Benbridge Show."

"Thanks a bunch, Tom." Jess shuddered, thinking about the most nerve-wracking experience she'd ever gone through.

Jess looked across the grass to where the stunt

riders were circling their mounts. *One... two... three...* She tried to count the timing in her head, but her thoughts were drowned out by the sound of blood pumping in her ears.

"Are we ready?" the director called. Jess looked across at Sarah, who smiled back at her confidently. Nodding, Jess turned her head and fixed her eyes straight ahead.

"And... ACTION!" the director yelled, as the clapperboard snapped shut.

Everything fell silent. Jess glanced across at the stunt riders, who were poised ready to go. Then she looked over to the film crew, seeing everyone's expectant faces staring at her. She tried to move her leg to nudge Storm Cloud on, but it felt like a dead weight hanging down. She fumbled with her reins, but they were all tangled up in her fingers.

Suddenly, Jess felt a wave of panic rushing through her body. "I– I– I'm not sure I can do this," she whispered. Storm Cloud shifted her weight. Nobody moved. "I'm not sure I can do this," she repeated, this time in a louder voice.

A murmur rippled through the crowd.

"CUT!" the director shouted.

Sarah glanced at the director, then hurried over to Jess. "Are you OK, Jess?" Sarah said, her voice full of concern. "What's up?"

Jess felt tears welling up in her eyes. "I-I just don't think I can do it," she whispered, her voice shaking. "What if I do something wrong, and Storm Cloud gets hurt – just like what happened with Bella and Skylark? I would never forgive myself."

Sarah looked up at Jess and smiled. "Jess, that's not going to happen. I wouldn't have suggested you do this unless I thought you were one hundred percent capable. I've seen you ride side-saddle and you're a natural. Just relax into it and try to forget the cameras are there."

Jess sighed. Slowly, she felt the tension release in her shoulders as Sarah's words began to sink in. *Sarah's right*, Jess thought. *I can do this.*

"You're just like I was at your age." Sarah smiled.

"All you need is a bit of confidence!"

Jess felt a warm glow in her cheeks and she smiled back at Sarah. Tightening up Storm Cloud's reins, she looked over to the director.

"OK, I'm ready!" she shouted.

Another murmur rippled through the crowd and the director nodded. Jess cantered Storm Cloud over to the right-hand side of the field. "OK." She gritted her teeth. "Let's show them, Storm Cloud."

The director raised his hand.

"AND... ACTION," he shouted. The clapperboard snapped shut again.

Jess pressed her thigh down into the side-saddle, and nudged Storm Cloud across the meadow. She felt the power surge beneath her as she asked the little pony for the speed. Checking her at the middle of the meadow, Jess went to turn...

Bother! She had missed her cue. She glanced across at the director, who was waving his hands in the air.

"CUT... CUT..." he shouted, shaking his head.

Feeling her face burning madly, Jess turned Storm Cloud back to the start. "Sorry guys," she mouthed to the chase riders, who were circling their mounts one more time. *Concentrate,* Jess told herself.

She took a deep breath and nodded at the director to start again.

"Let's do it again, please," the director shouted.

A few moments later, Jess and Storm Cloud were flying across the grass. Jess's heart thumped madly in her chest. As she reached the centre of the meadow, she began to count in her head. *One... two... three.* She looked over her shoulder, pushing Storm Cloud on faster and faster still.

Just then, out of the corner of her eye, Jess noticed the hedge where Skylark had fallen. She flinched, suddenly losing all her concentration. She'd missed the cue again.

"You missed it, Jess," the director called. "Let's try it one more time."

Jess nodded and circled Storm Cloud to turn her back to the start. *Just ignore the hedge,* she thought.

She could see her mum, who was looking anxiously from the fence. Jess had to get this right. For Sarah, for Sandy Lane, and for everyone who had come along to support her.

She and Storm Cloud stood ready. The stunt riders came to join her and the cameras rolled back across the ground. She took a deep breath, then the clapperboard came down and she was off again, nudging Storm Cloud across the grass.

This time, everything felt different. Jess felt in control. Storm Cloud did as she was asked, responding to Jess's aids with ease. *One... two... three...* Jess glanced back at the stunt riders, then pushed Storm Cloud into a gallop. Everything around her seemed to blur into one big smudge of green. As she pressed her thigh down into the side-saddle, Jess moved with Storm Cloud as one. Then, a few moments of sheer adrenaline later, Jess heard herself exhale, and Storm Cloud checked herself and began slowing down.

They'd done it! They'd reached the other side of

the meadow. This time, Jess hadn't even noticed the hedge where Skylark took her fall.

"CUT!" the director shouted. "Good job, Jess."

Jess's heart pounded as she trotted Storm Cloud back towards the fence, and a huge cheer rose up from the crowd.

"HIP HIP HOORAY!" came Rosie's voice through the applause.

She'd done it! The sound of clapping rang in Jess's ears. She carefully dismounted, feeling breathless and exhausted.

"Well done, Storm Cloud," Jess whispered.

"That was fantastic, Jess," the director called over to her. "You really nailed it."

Jess beamed, as Rosie rushed over to give her a big hug.

"I'm so proud of you, love," Jess's mother cried, jogging across the meadow with Sarah. "You looked like a proper stunt rider!"

"You certainly did," Sarah grinned, giving Jess a squeeze. "I couldn't have done it better myself."

"You looked awesome up there." Tom grinned, patting Jess on the back.

"Thanks! I guess it wasn't bad." Jess smiled. She took off her hat and shook out her messy brown hair. "It wasn't bad at all."

Chapter 14

The Final Cut

"I'll be with you in two minutes, Mum," Jess called, brushing her hair in front of the mirror.

"I've heard that before," Jess's mother called up from downstairs. "Come on!"

Jess smiled. This time it was different. She didn't want to be late for the preview screening of the film at Sandy Lane. It had been just over a month since filming had finished and Nick was holding a party at Sandy Lane to celebrate. Rob Fraser had given Nick a copy of Jess's unedited scenes, ahead of the film's release. Jess and Rosie had spent all afternoon decorating the tack room and Nick had even set up a large projector screen on the back wall, which linked up to his laptop.

Jess flicked out her hair and stepped out into the hallway. "I'm ready, Mum!"

"You look every bit the film star," Jess's mother said, appearing in the hall with the car keys. "I suppose that's why you're always fashionably late!"

A short ride later, Jess was walking up the drive into the yard. She could hear the excited voices ahead of her as she made her way to the tack room.

Jess grinned as she pushed open the door. All her friends were there – Rosie, Tom, Alex and even Izzy Paterson, who was back from her summer abroad. Nick was standing on a chair and fiddling with the lights, while Sarah was bouncing Zoe on her lap and calling out instructions from her seat.

"Look, Tom," Alex said, nudging his friend. "We're in the presence of fame!"

Tom crunched down on a mouthful of crisps, before jumping up to make an exaggerated bow. "It's an honour, ma'am," he teased.

Jess felt herself going red.

"Ignore them, Jess." Sarah laughed.

Pouring herself a glass of lemonade, Jess sat down next to Rosie and Izzy, and the girls launched into excited chatter.

It could only have been a few minutes later, when Jess noticed that the room had gone quiet. Everybody was staring at the door. Slowly, she turned around to see what everyone was looking at.

In the doorway stood a very pale-looking girl, leaning awkwardly on a pair of crutches. For a second, Jess wondered who on earth she was. Then she gasped. It was Bella! The teen star looked completely different now – barely recognizable in fact. Wearing a baggy grey sweatshirt, her brown hair was tied back roughly in a ponytail and she had a plaster cast on her leg, right up to her thigh.

"Hi Jess," Bella mumbled, hobbling in on her crutches. "Hello everyone."

"Welcome back, Bella," Sarah said, walking over

to the door to greet her. "Glad to see you on your feet again. I'm so pleased you made it tonight."

Bella smiled weakly; her face looked tired. "Thank you for the invite, Sarah. I know I'm probably the last person anyone wants to see." Bella glanced at Jess guiltily.

"Don't be silly," Sarah replied. "We're just happy to see you're recovering. Where's your mother?"

Bella stared at the ground. "I told Mom not to come. Rob brought me instead. He's just parking the car. My mom... she keeps insisting that it's Sandy Lane's fault... the accident... I had to make her promise not to get the courts involved."

Sarah frowned and opened her mouth to speak.

"It's OK, don't worry," Bella said quickly. "I told her it was completely my fault and she's finally dropped the subject."

"Well, that's a relief..." Sarah said nervously. "I'd hate her to think we were in any way responsible."

"It's just Mom's way of letting off steam," Bella went on. "Don't worry."

As everybody in the tack room began chatting to each other again, Jess looked at Bella curiously. She seemed so different now; all her haughtiness had gone. Now, she seemed like an ordinary girl – a bit shy, even.

Jess coughed, plucking up the courage to speak. "So, how are you feeling, Bella?" she asked.

"Yeah, not bad, thanks," Bella answered, turning towards her. Jess noticed that her eyes were shiny with tears. "Actually, I came to say goodbye. And... well, to thank you for filling in for my scenes... and, well, I'm *so* sorry about what happened to Skylark. It was totally my fault. I shouldn't have ridden that fast. It was so stupid."

At the mention of Skylark, Jess felt the anger bubbling up inside her.

"Then why did you do it, Bella?" she blurted out. "I trusted you to take care of Skylark. She might never have been able to walk again!"

A tear trickled down Bella's face. "I know it's unforgivable what I did, and I don't blame you if you never want to see me again..." Her voice began to crack. "I– I guess I was just trying to be more like you. You were so good at riding side-saddle, and you have so many friends. I don't have any – just fans who don't even know the real me. At the movie set that day, I just wanted to prove to everyone I could be as good as you..."

Jess sighed, thinking back to how Bella had acted around her. "I tried really hard to welcome you, but you kept knocking it back in my face."

Bella started sniffing, and Jess rummaged around in her pocket for a tissue. She couldn't believe it, but she was starting to actually feel sorry for the girl.

"I... I was trying to impress everyone, I guess," Bella mumbled, taking the tissue and blowing her nose. "People always have these expectations. And I don't know how to act around people so the easiest thing to do is put on a show."

Jess remembered the time Bella had walked into the tack room, to overhear Jess making fun of her. Instantly, she felt guilty.

"I suppose it must be difficult," Jess said quietly. "I'm sorry you felt you had to put on a show for us."

"So, can we be friends?" Bella held out her hand gingerly, resting the other on her crutch.

Jess sighed and took Bella's hand. "Friends," she said, leaning over to hug her.

"One more thing," Bella added. "Would you mind if I go to see Skylark? I've bought a treat for her, and I want to say sorry."

Jess smiled. Bella really did seem to have changed. "Of course," she replied. "She's doing really well. The vet says she's making good progress."

Just at that moment, there was a sound at the door. It was Rob Fraser, holding a large parcel.

"Sorry to interrupt, folks," he said, as the tack room fell quiet again. "I've got something for Jess." Turning to Jess, he held out a parcel ceremoniously. "On behalf of the whole film crew, please take this as a token of our thanks. If it wasn't for you, the movie might never have been finished," he said.

Jess laughed bashfully, taking the parcel from

Rob. It was really big and heavy and Jess had to rest it on the floor.

"Go on, Jess," Nick called out. "Open it."

Jess hesitated for a moment, then carefully began opening the parcel. An excited murmur rippled through the tack room. There, inside, was an original, polished leather side-saddle.

"Oh wow," Jess breathed, feeling the soft leather under her hands. "But I can't accept this," she said.

"Yes, you can," Rob said firmly. "If it wasn't for you, we'd be in all sorts of trouble. Not only that, but we want to make you an offer."

"An offer?" Jess whispered.

"Well, the director has asked me to pass on a message. He'd like it if you could help out in the sequel to the movie. Bella is already signed up, but we need another female rider to do the stunts alongside her. Filming is scheduled to start next summer. What do you say? Would you be interested?"

"You mean you want me to be a stunt rider in the film?" Jess said, looking at Rob in wonder.

"Yes." Rob smiled. "And, once Skylark's fully recovered, we were actually hoping you'll be able to ride her. Only if you want to, that is."

"Well, there is Colcott next year..." Jess began. Then, she beamed at Rob. "I'd absolutely love to!"

"Looks like Jess might become the world's leading stunt rider," Alex said, nudging Tom.

"Can I have your autograph, Jess?" Tom joked.

"I can't believe my best friend is going to be a film star!" Rosie cried.

"Right, on that note, I think it's time to watch the film," Nick said. "Take your seats, ladies and gents."

"It's only the uncut footage," Rob added. "You'll have to wait till next year to see the full version."

There was a murmur of excitement as everyone sat down. Nick dimmed the lights and the film began to roll.

First, there were lots of scenes with Bella and Skylark. Jess had to admit they looked good together. Everyone took a sharp breath as the camera zoomed in on Skylark, who looked utterly breathtaking as she galloped across the beach. Then it was Jess's scene – the big finale they'd all been waiting for. Everybody whooped as Jess and Storm Cloud flew across the meadow, the turf kicking out behind them. Jess could hardly recognize herself.

"Look at them go!" Tom cried, leaning forward in his seat.

It looked totally different to how it had felt doing the scene. At one point it seemed as though the riders were never going to catch her... And finally she was cornered in the meadow and the film cut to black. There was a short pause, before everyone in the tack room broke into a huge round of applause.

"Pretty good, eh?" Nick stood up. "That's homegrown Sandy Lane talent right there."

"Jess, you look amazing on screen," Rosie breathed. "I know you had to miss Colcott this year, but seriously – that performance was something else! You should win an Oscar!"

Jess laughed. "Bella is the real star of the show, I just helped out where I could." She turned to Bella and grinned. "So, Bella, do you want to come and say hello to Skylark?"

"I'd love to," Bella said. "Thank you."

Jess beckoned Bella towards the door, and the two girls slipped out into the night. Slowly, they walked across the yard towards Skylark's stable.

Jess felt a lump rise in her throat as she saw the familiar shape of her pony, looking over the door of her stable on the other side of the yard. Skylark let out a whinny of recognition.

"Hello there, little one," she said. "I've got someone here who wants to see you."

Bella reached into her pocket and pulled out some edible treats.

"I'm truly sorry for what I did, Skylark," she said, earnestly, holding out her hand as Skylark nibbled at the treats. "I hope you can forgive me."

Skylark let out a soft whinny and nuzzled under Bella's arm. Bella laughed, and let the pony rest there for a moment.

"I think that's her way of forgiving you," Jess said

gently, stroking Skylark's nose.

Bella smiled. "I'm so glad."

"You'd better hurry up and get better soon, girl." Jess looked at her pony fondly, as Skylark munched on Bella's treats. "We've got plenty in store for you when you're well again. Just you wait!"

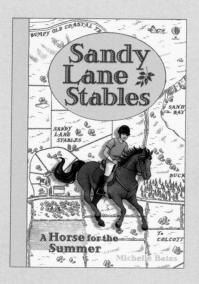

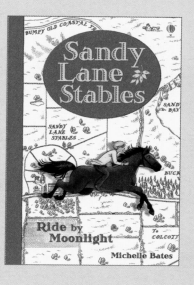

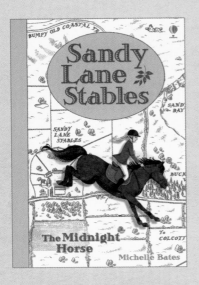

Sandy Lane Stables

The Midnight Horse

Michelle Bates

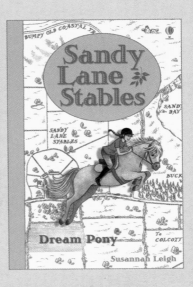

Sandy Lane Stables

Dream Pony

Susannah Leigh

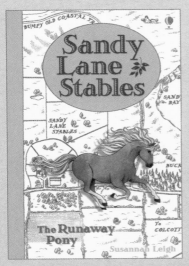

Sandy Lane Stables

The Runaway Pony

Susannah Leigh

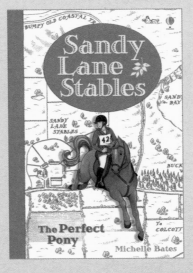

Sandy Lane Stables

The Perfect Pony

Michelle Bates